10 Minutes till Bedtime

PEGGY RATHMANN

PUFFIN BOOKS

PUFFIN BOOKS

Published by the Penguin Group
Penguin Books Ltd, 80 Strand, London WC2R 0RL, England
Penguin Putnam Inc., 375 Hudson Street, New York, New York 10014, USA
Penguin Books Australia Ltd, 250 Camberwell Road, Camberwell, Victoria 3124, Australia
Penguin Books Canada Ltd, 10 Alcorn Avenue, Toronto, Ontario, Canada M4V 3B2
Penguin Books India (P) Ltd, 11 Community Centre, Panchsheel Park, New Delhi – 110 017, India
Penguin Books (NZ) Ltd, Cnr Rosedale and Airborne Roads, Albany, Auckland, New Zealand
Penguin Books (South Africa) (Pty) Ltd, 24 Sturdee Avenue, Rosebank 2196, South Africa

Penguin Books Ltd, Registered Offices: 80 Strand, London WC2R 0RL, England

www.penguin.com

First published in the USA by G. P. Putnam's Sons, a division of Penguin Putnam Books for Young Readers, 1998
Published in Great Britain by Viking 2000
Published in Puffin Books 2001
3 5 7 9 10 8 6 4

Copyright © Peggy Rathmann, 1998
All rights reserved

The moral right of the author/illustrator has been asserted

Made and printed in Italy by Printer Trento Srl

Except in the United States of America, this book is sold subject to the condition that it shall not, by way of trade or otherwise, be lent,
re-sold, hired out, or otherwise circulated without the publisher's prior consent in any form of binding or cover other than that in which it is
published and without a similar condition including this condition being imposed on the subsequent purchaser

British Library Cataloguing in Publication Data
A CIP catalogue record for this book is available from the British Library

ISBN 0-140-56653-8

269944

P.3

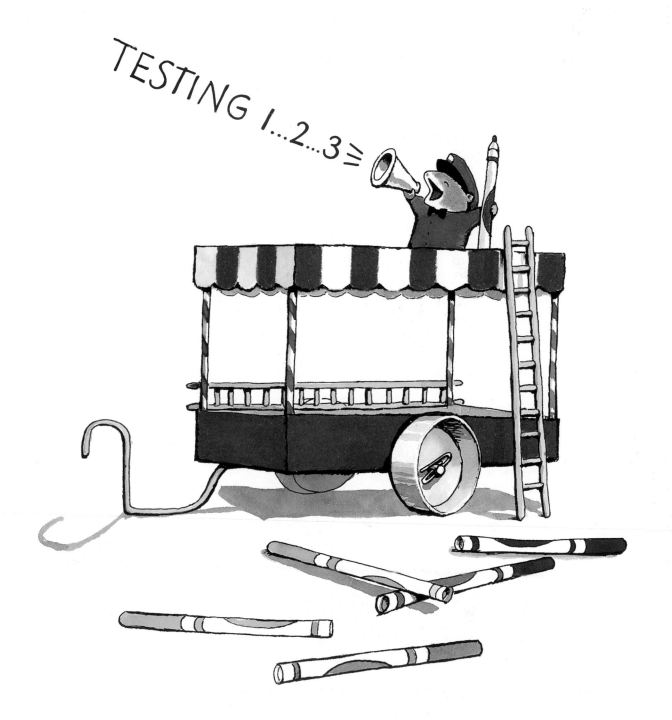

SEVEN MINUTES

toof

faster